TONY HAWK'S
900 revolution

VOLUME 6

Tony Hawk's 900 Revolution
is published by Stone Arch Books
a Capstone imprint, 1710 Roe Crest Drive, North Mankato,
MN 56003 www.capstonepub.com Copyright © 2012
by Stone Arch Books All rights reserved. No part of this
publication may be reproduced in whole or in part, or stored
in a retrieval system, or transmitted in any form or by any
means, electronic, mechanical, photocopying, recording, or
otherwise, without written permission of the publisher.

Cataloging-in-Publication Data is available on the Library
of Congress website.
ISBN: 978-1-4342-3312-7 (library binding)
ISBN: 978-1-4342-3888-7 (paperback)

Summary: As the Revolution team secures more pieces
of Tony Hawk's 900 skateboard, the skills of each
member are suddenly magnified. For Omar Grebes, this
surge of power equals a flood of psychic visions about
the locations of the Artifacts and the origin of their
mysterious powers. He's determined to find the rest of the
missing pieces as fast as possible. Unfortunately, Omar's
worldwide search quickly leads to a whirlwind of trouble
for the team.

Photo and Vector Graphics Credits: Shutterstock.
Photo credit page 122, Bart Jones/ Tony Hawk.

Art Director: Heather Kindseth
Cover and Interior Graphic Designer: Kay Fraser
Comic Insert Graphic Designer: Hilary Walcholz

Printed in the United States of America in Stevens Point,
Wisconsin.
102011
006404WZS12

TONY HAWK'S 900 revolution

TUNNEL VISION

BY BRANDON TERRELL // ILLUSTRATED BY CAIO MAJADO

VOLUME 6

STONE ARCH BOOKS
a capstone imprint

1

"Bird One to Nest: I've got the Fragment, but I'm not flying solo anymore."

Omar Grebes pushed hard and leaned forward. His skateboard rattled over the narrow, moonlit streets of Venice, Italy. The wiry fifteen-year-old hazarded a glance over his shoulder. Two teens dressed head to toe in black, with night-vision goggles obscuring their faces, pursued him on skateboards of their own.

"Copy that, Bird One," a voice crackled in the sleek earpiece fastened inside Omar's helmet. "Are they Collective agents?"

"Yeah. Angry ones."

"Okay. We've got your location, and we'll guide you back to the nest."

That was the best news Omar could hear, and he silently thanked the GPS tracking watch he wore on his wrist.

The city of Venice was built on an interconnected series of waterways called canals. The long, winding streets and passages had a tendency to end abruptly, and boats were the main source of transportation through the city. It was enough to make even the most experienced navigator lost and claustrophobic. Omar was just a kid from SoCal, and he wasn't the greatest with following directions. Right now, he felt like that ancient Greek dude, Theseus, trapped in a labyrinth with a couple of Minotaurs on his tail.

"Canal fifty feet ahead," the voice in Omar's ear directed. "Take a hard right."

Omar spotted the waterway before him, illuminated by a pool of light from a streetlamp. He quickly performed a frontside 180 and rode goofy, with his right foot in front. He crouched low and dug into the heel side of the board. Leaning back, he supported his weight by clutching the deck with his left hand and gliding his right hand along the uneven road, carving around a crumbling stone structure in a tight turn.

"Now that's a thing of beauty," Omar said proudly. "Let's see those Collective boys do that."

Omar was a world-renowned skateboarder, but he knew his skill tonight was not solely his own. The board beneath his feet produced a steady, rich blue glow. Its uncanny power stemmed from one of the front wheels, a Fragment of the legendary Tony Hawk 900 skateboard. Omar had discovered the wheel at the murky bottom of the Pacific Ocean, near the islands of Todos Santos. Since then, Omar had become one member in a team of skilled teens who were searching the world for the Fragments — like the one nestled in the side pocket of his cargo pants. It was one half of a skateboard truck axle from the 900 board. Tonight's recovery was supposed to be simple. Retrieve the Fragment and get out clean. Until the Collective goons behind him had showed up and screwed it up royally.

Still, Omar had the Fragment. It radiated power, glowing blue and crackling with electricity beneath the khaki fabric of his pocket. With his deck beneath his feet, Omar could almost feel his heartbeat, reaction time, and speed quicken just by having the Fragments near him. It was a rush like no other.

In front of him, the pathway widened, and Omar shot out into a large, open plaza. He remembered this place from the pre-mission briefing and Eldrick's fancy satellite photos: Piazza San Marco.

During the day, the plaza swarmed with tourists, vendors, and pigeons. Omar wouldn't have been able to even stand on his board. But in the middle of the night, the place was nearly bare. Omar sped through the plaza, weaving around a pair of romantic lovebirds holding hands and startling them. The man waved a fist at Omar and yelled what were probably curse words in Italian at him.

"Look alive, you've got more company," the voice in his earpiece commanded.

Omar looked back for the two skaters pursuing him. He saw them riding around a stone column and making their way into the plaza. They were no match for him. Omar was leaving them in his concrete wake, and he didn't see any additional Collective agents.

That was when he heard it.

The hum of an engine.

A small motocross bike roared from the shadows to his left. On it sat a third Collective agent. This teen, however, meant business. In his left hand was a tranquilizer gun. The agent raised the gun, pointing it at Omar.

As quick as he could, Omar ducked behind a marble fountain. He heard the sharp sound of tranq darts impacting with the stone and shattering.

"Little help here!" Omar shouted.

"We're already on it, Bird One. Fly left around the Basilica San Marco, then another left into the city. Stay in tight, enclosed spaces. He'll be forced to slow down. There's a reason they don't allow vehicles in Venice."

"Got it."

Omar did as he was instructed, pushing as hard as his tired legs could manage. When his energy began to fade, the Fragment on his board picked up the slack. *Better than an energy drink*, Omar thought.

The teen on the motorcycle holstered the tranq gun and held onto his handlebars. He rode up beside Omar, swerving left in an attempt to get Omar to bail.

"Not happening, bro," Omar said, shoving the rider hard with both hands. The two split apart.

Before them, a wide canal cut across their path. A bridge, staggered with steps, arched over the water. Omar picked up his pace, dug down for a burst of energy, leaned back, and ollied high into the air. The back truck of his board locked onto the white guardrail of the bridge halfway up. His momentum propelled him forward, and he performed a perfect frontside nosegrind across the rail and back down the other side.

He landed on the stone walkway, quickly looking for the motorcyclist.

The bike had vanished.

"I think I lost him," Omar said, finding a groove and speeding along the concourse with ease.

He was not alone for long. Another motorcycle darted out from behind a building to Omar's left, heading directly for him. Omar shoved hard with his back foot, bringing the board to a stuttering stop and shredding its tail. Not expecting Omar's abrupt move, the motorcycle shot past him. Its rider quickly cranked the handlebars left, the back tire skidding and the smell of burnt rubber filling Omar's nostrils.

Omar pushed hard, trying to build speed quickly and gain some distance from the motorcycle. Without warning, the cobalt glow emanating from his pocket encompassed him, shot up his spine and into his head.

He sees mountains. Sunlight. The ocean. A blinding light plummeting from the sky, almost too bright to see. It crashes through foliage, and hits the earth with a shuddering rumble. Birds erupt from the trees. The ground quakes. A large snake, black as oily night, slithers up the side of the mountain, searching for the iridescent object from the sky. Boulders cascade down the rocky terrain in its wake. A brown and black bird gracefully swoops in, flapping its wings at the viper. The angry snake coils, prepares to strike.

And then he was whipped back from the vision. He was on the ground, his face mashed in gritty earth. He could feel the road rash on his left arm, a throbbing pain above his elbow pad. He'd tumbled from his board. *Could have been worse*, he thought, straightening the helmet on his head. *Thank you, helmet.*

It had been a while since he'd had a vision, and even then, it was not like this. This was painful. Almost . . . real.

"Come in, Bird One," the static, hollow voice sounded in his ear.

"I'm here," Omar said. He shook his head, trying to clear it, to focus on getting away from the Collective safely. He raised himself up onto his hands and knees, saw his board ten feet away. "Where's that help?" he asked as he staggered to his feet.

A tranq dart whizzed past Omar's ear, close enough to feel the breeze. He whipped around. The second motorcyclist had stopped as the first pulled up beside him. They were angrily shouting at one another. The second teen was leveling his tranquilizer gun again, with Omar in the crosshairs.

This time, there was nowhere to hide.

2

"Sorry I'm late!" Joey Rail's voice erupted from Omar's earpiece as, from out of nowhere, a charcoal gray BMX bike soared through the air. It landed in front of Omar just as the Collective agent fired his weapon. The tranq dart bounced harmlessly off the back of Joey's Kevlar vest. Despite the dark, Omar was almost positive he could see his friend's wide grin beneath the protective shield of the helmet.

"You're a sight for sore eyes, Rail," Omar said.

Joey pedaled up beside Omar.

"Latch on," Joey said. "Let's take a midnight stroll."

Omar rushed over to his fallen board, snatched it up, and ran. Dropping the deck, he leaped on.

Omar's skate shoe scraped the ground as he pushed off and rode faster. A chrome handlebar extended from the back of Joey's black seat. Omar grabbed it and held tight as the BMX took off. He could hear the motorcycles revving and continuing their pursuit.

"Hey, Omar," Joey said.

"Yeah?"

"Why are you making new friends? Don't you like the ones you've got?"

Joey laughed at his own joke, enjoying the sense of danger and excitement. Omar was too distracted by the lingering feeling he'd received with his vision to banter with his friend. The added intensity of his premonition had to have come from the newest Fragment, from the truck axle resting in his pocket. He had to be rid of it, before he became a danger to himself and Joey.

The salty air whipped past Omar's face as the two rocketed along the walkway, dipping in and out of the streetlamps' glow. Without looking behind him, though, Omar could sense the motorcycles gaining on them.

"We need to split up," Omar directed, pointing Joey to a small plaza tucked further back in the city. A towering church stood draped in shadows, and a wide canal cut through the middle of the open plaza. Joey swung the bike in a hard left.

Omar released his grip on the chrome bar, gliding along the left side of the canal. Joey directed his bike to the right side, crossing a pedestrian bridge.

Omar dug into his pocket and withdrew the powerful piece of skateboard. The plaza was suddenly bathed in the Fragment's blue light. He ran his thumb over the rough, scratched metal, the clean split down its middle. *The other half is still out there*, he thought.

"Fragment's coming, Rail," Omar said. "Look alive."

Still moving at a good clip, Omar cocked his right arm back like a star quarterback, and flung the Fragment in the air. It spun end over end. He didn't worry about the artifact. He knew its power would safely guide it to Joey. A thin strand of blue electricity arced across the sky as the Fragment passed over the canal, toward the waiting BMX rider.

A sudden, forceful shock of electricity coursed its way from the truck, back along the arc, to Omar's still outstretched right hand. A jolt of pain engulfed and dug into his palm, and his arm went numb.

"Ah!" Omar cried out in pain. He lost control of his deck, careening across the cobblestone walkway. The front wheel of his board hit a gap in the stone. Omar was airborne, flying across the sky, over the side of the path, and into the murky depths of the canal.

3

Tommy. The snake is Tommy. His best friend — no, closer than that, more like his brother — is trying to kill him. Omar is on the mountain, has transformed from the bird back into a human. The sun burns his face. Tommy is standing over him. It is just the two of them at the pinnacle of the mountain, the only remaining members of a once-close family. Zeke is dead. Tommy has betrayed him. Omar is alone. Tommy lifts off the ground, seems to hover over Omar. How is he doing that? Omar looks down. Tommy's legs are gone. In their place is the fat, coiled body of the black snake. A blinding light erupts, and Tommy has vanished. In his place is a symbol, something Omar has not seen before. Triangular, with the profile of a bird, beak open, wings tucked at its side, diving downward. Below it, letters.

They are nothing Omar can read, ancient symbols more like hieroglyphics than English. He tries to remember it before . . . The blinding light burns again, and the symbol is nothing but a watermark on his eyes. Omar sees his hand, clutching a rock, holding on for dear life. Another hand reaches down and grabs his wrist. It is dirty, scabbed. He knows he should feel safe, but he does not. The hand is not his salvation; it is his doom. A snake slithers down the dirty hand as it pries Omar's fingers off the rock, and releases him. Omar is falling. He is weightless. He is —

— sinking to the bottom of the canal. The sting of saltwater greeted him as he opened his eyes and clawed for the nonexistent mountainside in his vision. Omar opened his mouth to yell, and the dirty water rushed in, choked him, forced him to cough even when he couldn't. He heard a splash and saw a figure cutting through the darkness toward him. He reached up for it, and realized his right arm, the one struck by the electric blast, was not responding. It was still numb.

When the figure reached Omar, it wrapped its arms around his torso and began to kick toward the surface. Omar's lungs ached. He needed to breathe, but his lungs were filled with saltwater. They rose toward the surface, but it felt as if they would never make it.

Yet they did. Omar felt the cool night air against his face as he broke the surface and gasped for breath. He retched and spat out the muddy seawater, coughing violently.

Beside him in the water was a caramel-dreadlocked beauty. It was Neelu, the teenage girl he had befriended when he joined the Revolution. She was a stunning beauty, even in the filth of a Venice canal at night.

"Are you all right?" Neelu asked.

Omar took a moment to regain his breath. "Yeah," he said.

"Aren't grebes supposed to be at home in the water?"

"Apparently just the ones with beaks."

"You know, this is the second time I've saved your butt from drowning," Neelu informed him as she swam toward a waiting motorboat. "I hope you're not making it a habit."

"At least there was no mouth-to-mouth this time," Omar muttered.

Neelu smiled. "Yeah, well . . ."

Neelu and Omar started to swim toward the boat. His right arm felt like it was being pricked by thousands of needles, like it had been asleep and was just now waking up.

A rope ladder splashed into the water from the boat.

Warren Rafe, the man behind the voice in Omar's earpiece and one of the leaders of the Revolution, leaned over the side of the craft.

"Are you okay, Grebes?" There was a genuine look of concern in the twenty-five-year-old's almond eyes. He was aware of Omar's battle with hydrophobia, and had hesitations about sending the teen out alone to retrieve the Fragment in the first place because of it. "It's a city built on water," he'd argued. "There's no way this will end well."

"Yeah . . . fine," Omar answered.

"Well, you're lucky we were close." Rafe reached out and helped Neelu climb up the ladder and into the boat. Omar followed, using his left hand to haul himself up onto the ladder. He held out his right hand, noticing for the first time a blistering sore in his palm, about the size of a silver dollar, from where the Fragment's electric blast had struck him. As Rafe pulled Omar safely up the ladder, the teen closed his hand into a fist, hiding the injury from his superior.

Dripping wet, Omar slogged his way onto the boat. He peeled the shaggy brown hair off his forehead as a crisp white towel smacked him in the chest.

"So much for your James Bond audition," Dylan Crow said.

The New York skater, nicknamed Slider, sat in the back of the boat. He wore his ever-present Yankees baseball cap, its flat bill cranked to the left and pulled so low Omar could not see the cocky loner's eyes.

"Leave him be, Dylan," Amy Kestrel, the final member of the team, said from her perch beside Slider. She playfully swatted at Slider, who dodged her hand.

"Where's Joey?" Omar asked. His throat felt raw from swallowing and coughing up saltwater.

"Three canals over, and moving fast," Rafe said as he studied a small screen positioned to the right of the boat's steering wheel. Joey's voice crackled in Rafe's earpiece, and Omar instinctively reached for his own ear. The device was no longer there, his helmet lost at the bottom of the canal. Hoping that the gadget was not the only item lost for good, Omar quickly scanned the stone ground where he'd toppled into the canal.

Intuiting what Omar was looking for, Neelu said, "We have your board. It's safe." She nodded her head to the rear of the boat, where the battered skateboard rested.

"We're heading to the rendezvous point," Rafe informed Joey in the earpiece.

Omar sat in a plush seat next to Rafe and wrapped the towel around his body. "And the Fragment?"

"Joey still has it," Neelu answered as she sat beside him, drying her dreads with a towel of her own.

Omar noticed Neelu shivering, and draped his own towel over her shoulders.

Rafe fired up the boat's inboard motor, its sound echoing along the stone walls of the plaza.

The team followed the winding canals for what felt like an eternity. Omar kept a vigilant eye out for any Collective agents, but their route was clear. At long last, they reached the city's main canal — the Lido di Venezia — a massive waterway that wound through the city and eventually into the Adriatic Sea. They were not the only boat on the main thoroughfare this late at night. Water taxis trolled slowly past them, as well as the occasional motorboat or gondola. All were oblivious to the dangerous action happening around them. Rafe leaned heavily on the boat's throttle, churning up a killer wake. Omar could tell the man wanted to get the heck out of Dodge. He did, too.

"So Venice is considered the most romantic city on Earth, right?" Slider asked as they passed a gondola occupied with a canoodling couple.

"Yeah," Amy answered. "Why?"

"Just trying to figure out how someone could fall in love in a place that smells like a dirty aquarium."

"Oh, and New York smells like roses?" Amy asked.

"Well it certainly doesn't smell like fish, Miss Colorado."

"Quiet, you two," Rafe said, silencing Slider and Amy's playful bickering. He was studying the thin, GPS-locating device attached to the boat's steering column. Omar craned his neck to see the screen as Rafe pulled the boat alongside a small pier. A line of tall, crumbling stone buildings stood twenty feet from their location in the canal. A rectangular sign on one of the buildings read 'Calle de Falco,' referring to the narrow passage between two structures.

"Where's our boy?" Slider asked.

"Closing in," Rafe answered without taking his eyes from the screen.

Omar stared at the buildings blanketed in shadow. Stretched from one building to the window of another was a clothesline. On it, an array of colorful garments whipped about in the night breeze.

Then, from the shadows, Joey's BMX shot from the thin gap between buildings, jumping off a concrete slab and getting major air. Joey twisted his bike up until it was parallel with the ground, performing a solid tabletop trick, then landed smoothly and braked at the edge of the pier.

Joey unlatched and removed his helmet, adorned with a painted black and brown feather from his namesake, the Rail. His Cheshire Cat grin spread from ear to ear as he ruffled his sweaty, blonde hair.

"Hey, guys," Joey asked. "What are you waiting for?"

"Show-off," Slider said.

"Where are the Collective agents?" Rafe asked in a no-nonsense tone.

Joey leaped off his bike, nodding in the direction of the called he just emerged from. "One is eating concrete. The other is taking a dip like Omar did." He locked eyes with the soaked teen. "You good, O?"

Omar nodded. The tingle in his right hand was still there. Had Joey seen the blast of energy that had led to Omar taking a swim and nearly dying? If he had, he was keeping his mouth closed about it.

While Slider and Amy loaded the BMX bike on the boat and strapped it down, Joey plucked the truck Fragment from his pocket. Its radioactive pulsation increased, the cobalt glow deepening and thin tendrils of electricity enveloping the piece. Omar could sense the team's individual Fragments picking up on the pulse and humming like tuning forks.

Joey passed the metal axle to Rafe. "Don't say I never give you anything pretty," he joked.

Rafe did not laugh, instead securing the 900 Fragment in a lead-lined box before passing it off to Neelu for safekeeping. He then cranked the steering wheel hard starboard and gunned the throttle. Joey barely had time to sit before the boat began to rocket across the glassy surface of the canal.

On the horizon, Omar saw a stretch of land, and the twinkling lights of Venice's Marco Polo Airport. He thought of the Revolution's Black Hawk helicopter waiting there to take them home. His muscles, knotted from stress all night, suddenly loosened, and he felt himself growing increasingly tired.

He couldn't wait to sleep the whole way home.

4

Built amidst the desert landscape outside of Phoenix, Arizona were a smattering of abandoned warehouses, a junk heap, and a long-forgotten rail yard. The area was an eye sore. There wasn't a passerby on the interstate that would give the dilapidated, graffiti-tagged buildings a second glance. Which is exactly what the 900 Revolution team wanted.

One of the buildings, a long three-story structure with corrugated tin sides and a single, small entrance at the back, hid the team's location from the world. Its inside was outfitted with state of the art equipment, a top-notch training facility, and a centralized housing unit where the Revolution team ate, slept, and studied.

Omar sat on a cold, metal table in the facility's infirmary. Eldrick Otus, the silver-haired leader of the Revolution, scrutinized the burn on Omar's hand.

"This was caused by the Fragment?" Eldrick asked.

"Yeah," Omar answered. "It was like being struck by lightning. I lost feeling in my arm for a while, too."

"I've never seen anything like this before. A Fragment striking a Key . . . it's unheard of."

"Well, my hand would beg to differ."

Eldrick scoured a nearby table until he found ointment, a cotton swab, a square bandage, and a roll of white tape. As he began to dress Omar's injury, he said, "Have your visions become more focused? More vivid?"

Omar had not told anyone of the startling, intense visions he'd had in Italy. "Um . . ." he started.

Eldrick already knew the answer.

"Yeah," Omar finally admitted. "Major league visions. They felt almost real."

Eldrick nodded. "That's what I was afraid of."

"Wait, so you knew this would happen?"

"No." Eldrick applied the bandage and began to wrap Omar's hand in the smooth, white tape. "It was an assumption that has unfortunately proven true."

"Sounds like semantics, old man," Omar said. "Give it to me straight."

"As you've seen —" Eldrick indicated the pulsating wheel attached to Omar's deck, which leaned against a nearby chair, "— each Fragment of the 900 board comes with an alarming amount of power. It's easy to manage, and simple to control. However, as our mission progresses, the bonds between your friends and the Fragments are strengthening. And so is their potential."

"The more pieces we find, the stronger we become?"

"Yes."

"And my visions will only get worse?"

"They'll become more specific, yet uncontrolled." Eldrick wrapped the final strip of white tape around Omar's wrist. "Now, do you remember what you saw?"

"How could I forget?" Omar told Eldrick of the blinding light, the mountain, and the snake. He wasn't sure why, but he decided to keep Tommy's identity as the serpent in his vision a secret.

Eldrick became visibly uncomfortable when Omar mentioned the symbol carved in rock.

"Where was this carving? Did you recognize the symbol?"

Omar shrugged. "I've never seen it before."

"Do you remember what it looked like?"

"Sure." Omar reached into the pocket of his board shorts and removed a ballpoint pen.

The immediate vicinity failed to provide a scrap of paper to write on so, improvising, Omar began to scribble the symbol on the white-taped palm of his injured hand. The sketch was rudimentary, as Omar was right-handed, but when he was finished, the image was clear enough to decipher.

"There should be letters here," Omar drew a line below the base of the triangle. "Like . . . glyphs or something. But I don't remember what they were. I couldn't tell you what they meant anyway."

"Fascinating." Eldrick examined the triangular shape, the diving bird of prey with its beak open and wings tucked. He shook his head. "This is a question for the Elders," he whispered, mostly to himself.

"The Elders?" Omar asked.

Eldrick was taken aback that Omar had heard his whispers. "It's not your concern, son," he said.

Omar hopped off the table, straightened his T-shirt, and kicked his deck up and into his uninjured hand.

"If you don't mind, let's keep this information between us for the time being," Eldrick said.

"Yeah, okay."

"There's one last thing," Eldrick said, stopping Omar before the teen could reach the door.

"Yeah?"

"I think it would be best if you . . . stayed back for a while, just until you're able to control your visions."

"Wait. So I'm . . . what? Grounded?" Omar laughed at the idea.

"Well, yes, I suppose."

"What?! You can't ground me!" His humorous tone was gone, now replaced with borderline anger.

"Then consider it a suspension. Omar, if the events in Venice proved anything, it's that the power you wield is dangerous. You were nearly killed out there because of it. The next time you experience a vision, you may not get so lucky. I'm only doing what's best for the team."

"Yeah, sure. Whatever," Omar grumbled as he strode to the door. He tried to control his anger, but it got the best of him. The blue electricity from the wheel intensified, engulfed his board, and shot up his good arm. With a sizzling snap, Omar shoved the door open. For the briefest of moments, the blue glow was replaced by a deep shade of crimson. A flicker, and then it was gone.

Omar needed to vent his frustration, and the best way he knew how to do that was on his board. He dropped the glowing deck onto the concrete, hopped on, and glided along the hallway toward the training area.

As he rode, he thought of the conversation he'd just had with Eldrick. The Revolution leader's command should not have bothered the teen as much as it had. He should be cool with riding the pine for a while and letting the rest of the crew handle things without him, instead of sticking his neck out and putting his life on the line again. But the events he had seen in his vision were weighing heavily on him. He needed to be out there. Especially if it meant facing Tommy again.

The last time he had seen his best friend, they had been under the surface of the Pacific Ocean, fighting over the cream-colored wheel now rolling under Omar's feet. He still found it hard to believe that his enemy, one of the greatest threats to the world, was the same Tommy who used to sleep over at Omar's place, watching skating videos and munching on snack food and caffeine all night. The same Tommy who'd once made Omar laugh so hard milk and bits of cereal shot out of his nostrils. Omar had defeated Tommy, had watched as his older friend's body drifted unconscious down to the dismal depths of the muddy ocean floor. He had come to terms with the fact that Tommy was most likely dead by his hand. But according to his visions, the traitor had survived. This knowledge, however ominous it may be, also relieved Omar a bit. It meant he was not a murderer.

As Omar neared the vast, open area that contained the facility's training area, a bass-thumping beat filled the air. It rattled the windows and rumbled deep in his gut. Someone had let Slider choose the music today.

Awesomesauce, he sarcastically thought.

The hallway was on the second level of the facility, and at the end was a staircase and a wide landing that overlooked the training grounds.

Omar braked, kicked his board up into his hands, and leaned against the landing's waist-high guardrail.

The training area was a skater's dream. Against one wall was a full-pipe, colorfully tagged with some of Slider's signature 'artwork.' Next to it was an empty, kidney-shaped pool. A dirt BMX track, designed and maintained by Joey, wrapped around both. Against the wall was a three-story rock-climbing wall the team had dubbed the Beast.

Amy was about halfway up the wall. Around her waist was a black harness. A thick, yellow rope snaked from the harness, through a device attached to the ceiling, and down to the floor, where Joey, a mountain climber and an expert of all things outdoor, stood with his feet spread out for support. Slider stood next to him, board in hand. Both boys looked up at Amy.

"You're doing great, Amy!" Joey said.

"Man, that's the quickest I've ever seen you scale the Beast!" Slider added.

Omar descended the stairs, watching as Amy dug her feet into the toeholds and gracefully leaped into the air. It was a surprising move for someone as calculated about her technique as Amy. She reached out, locking the fingers of her left hand into a new hold higher up on the wall. Her feet naturally found new holds, as well.

"You're making it look easy!" Joey said.

"I feel like a different person!" Amy shouted down. "Like a pro!"

Slider dropped his board, hopped on it, and pushed off toward the pool. He cupped his hands around his mouth and shouted to Amy, "Now you know how I feel every day, Ames!"

Omar watched as Slider hit the pool edge and deftly performed a long backside smith grind on the pool's lip. With the front of the board already pointed downward, he dropped into the curved pool, gaining speed, coming up the side near Omar. He soared high and completed a solid 540. Omar saw the twisting underside of Slider's board, the black decal of the Brooklyn Bridge splattered with graffiti tags. He also saw the deck's different tail — the one from the Birdman's 900 board attached to Slider's during Dylan's run-in with the Collective in New York — and the blue glow emanating from it.

"Hey, O. What's the glum face for?" Joey had noticed Omar approaching. He offered Amy more slack in the rope as Omar walked over to join him.

Omar shrugged. "Just tired, I guess."

"Are you seeing what our girl can do?" Joey motioned his head at Amy.

"Hey, Omar," Amy called down, releasing one hand and waving. "You want a shot at the Beast?"

Omar shook his head. "Nah, not with my bum digits." He waggled his wrapped hand in the air. "I'm going to go get some rest. I'm still pretty drained."

"How's the hand?" Joey asked.

"Little road rash. Should be fine."

He hated lying to the team, but they'd know the truth soon enough. The way Amy was scaling the wall, and the way Slider was cranking out sick moves with ease? The Fragment's enhanced powers were already affecting them.

"Later, guys," Omar said as he walked toward the facility's sleeping quarters for what he thought would be peace, quiet, and maybe some shut-eye.

He was wrong.

6

The vision hit Omar before he had even flicked the lights on in his room. He felt himself falling toward his bed and then —

He's back on the mountain, plummeting to his death. He claws at the rock face as it whips by, trying to find a handhold. Nothing can save him. He is all alone now. His hands become brown and black feathers. He looks up to see the narrow wings of a brownish-red bird circling above him. He does not recognize the creature. He feels like he can fly. But to where? The blinding flash sends him off the mountain, upward. Looking down at an island from high above. He is mistaken. It is not a mountain. It is a volcano. The grouping of islands are easily recognizable: Hawaii.

The light flashes, and he is in a jungle. Then again, in a cold, swirling snow and a biting wind that will freeze exposed skin in seconds. They come fast — places, coordinates, images of blinding trails of light hitting the earth. They are Fragments. He is seeing their locations. It feels like a thousand places at once, like he's touring the globe on fast forward. The symbol is there; the symbol was always there. He just hadn't known where to find it . . .

Omar inhaled deeply, breathing in nothing but the unwashed sheets on his unmade bed. How long had he been out? It was hard to tell. Judging by the thin trail of fresh drool down the side of his face, not long.

He staggered to his feet. Under the white tape and bandage, his right hand itched and tingled. He flicked on the lights. The harsh glare of the overhead bulb forced him to squint as he shuffled through the drawers of a small metal desk. He was looking for paper. Sure, the images seared in his mind were not likely to fade like those in a normal dream. Still, he wasn't going to take any chances.

He found an old blue composition notebook and a pen, and furiously began to draw.

* * *

"Whoa, dude, what the heck happened in here?"

Omar jolted awake at the sound of Joey's voice. He sat at the desk, his forehead resting on the cool metal surface. He remembered drawing for what had felt like an eternity, until his hand muscles cramped up and he could hardly hold the pen anymore. He had just wanted to close his eyes for a second.

Mission failed.

Omar wiped the sleep from the corner of his eyes. Joey stood in the doorway, his jaw nearly needing a spatula to pry it up off the floor. "Talk about a strange art project, man," Joey said.

Omar's walls were filled with pages ripped from the composition book. Each piece of lined paper contained a drawing, a map of sorts. Some sported lists of numbers, the latitude and longitude of unfound Fragments. Omar had even found a folded map of the world in an ancient atlas and tacked it to the wall. Red lines trailed from a drawing to the map, with the location circled. Paris. New Zealand. Even Antarctica.

"Hey," Omar said quietly.

"Sorry. I knocked, but you were sleeping and the door was open. I just . . ."

"It's okay. Come in and close the door."

Joey did as Omar asked.

Joey nervously fidgeted with the cobra-braided bracelet on his wrist — a green parachute cord given to him by his dad, who was now stationed in Afghanistan.

"So what's up, Omar?" Joey asked.

"It's my head, Rail."

"Your head? Wait, does this have something to do with whatever happened in Venice? When you took that hit and belly-flopped into the stanky water?"

So Joey had seen the incident. No use hiding anything from him. Omar nodded. "Yeah. Lately, my visions have been . . . intense."

Joey nodded. "That's an understatement."

"I saw all of this, Rail. In visions."

"What are they?"

"I'm pretty sure these are the locations of all the other Fragments." His eyes flicked to a cluster of scribbled pages on the wall above his bed. They were images of Hawaii, of the volcano in his vision, the one where he and Tommy were destined to meet again.

"It makes sense, though," Joey said.

Omar furrowed his brow. "How so?"

"Something's different. We're all feeling it, man. You saw Amy on the Beast. It's like we're amped up." Joey stood. His hand reached for his Fragment, a ball bearing dangling around his neck.

He walked over to the cluster of Hawaiian images and scrutinized one closely. "So have you told Eldrick about your artwork yet?"

"No. It just happened."

"He's going to want to see this."

"Yeah, I know." Omar sighed heavily. "He sidelined me today."

"Because of your hand?"

"And my head. Until I get this —" He indicated the room's new wallpaper. "— figured out, he's not letting me out of this place."

"Sorry to hear it. So, I came to tell you, the flirtastic duo and I are heading into town for some grub. Maybe pizza and arcade games at Galaxy 'Za. You want me to score some ham and pineapple for you?"

Omar shook his head. "Thanks, but I'm going to get some rest, then probably forage for some nosh here."

"Cool." Joey walked to the door, stopped and turned back. "Omar, you know we've got your back, right?"

"Yeah." He wanted to answer sincerely, but he still had reservations. Omar remembered his vision, recalled the sensation of falling and knowing there was no one there to save him.

The feeling stuck with him until long after Joey had left.

Omar knew he shouldn't be doing what he was about to do, but he couldn't take it any longer. He'd been staring at the sketches of Hawaii for hours, formulating a plan that would defy Eldrick and possibly get him kicked off the Revolution team for good. But he had to know. About the symbol. About the Fragment. And especially about Tommy.

Omar quickly crammed his backpack with extra clothes and toiletries. He peeled the sketches of the Hawaiian Islands from his wall, folded them, and slid them into the front pocket of the pack.

"Stay radical, right?" he whispered to a vintage surfboard leaning against the wall beside his bed.

The two-word phrase was a Zeke specialty, and by saying it, Omar felt like his father was always with him.

The board, a 1965 Greg Noll Slot Bottom, was a gift from Eldrick. The turquoise-green board was the very same model his father, Zeke, had been riding the day he died. *The day Tommy killed him,* Omar reminded himself.

Before leaving, Omar unclasped the GPS-tracking watch from his wrist, and placed it in the bottom drawer of his desk. Then, with a deep breath, he snatched up his skateboard and left.

The facility was quiet this late in the evening. The trio of Revolution teens were probably in a wicked dance-off at the arcade right now, and Eldrick and Neelu had mentioned going into the city for supplies. That left Rafe as the only person he might encounter on his way out.

Omar could hear music emanating from the open door of the facility's weight room. Along with the music was the rhythmic sound of boxing gloves striking a punching bag. Perfect. Rafe was working out, and Omar was going to have to sneak past the weight room's open door in order to leave. He quietly made his way down the hall.

When he was just about to the door, a phone began to ring. Omar's heart leaped into his throat.

He clawed at the smartphone in his pocket. He was relieved to discover it was not his phone ringing, but Rafe's. He heard Rafe rip off his gloves and answer it.

"Yeah?" came Rafe's voice.

Omar peered into the weight room. It was filled with weights, a couple of treadmills, and an exercise bike. In the middle of the room was a black speed bag and a battered red punching bag. The punching bag still swayed on its chain from Rafe's workout.

Rafe stood shirtless and sweaty near a set of lockers lining the far wall. His back was to Omar as he talked in a conspiratorial tone on his phone.

"I agree, sir. We have not told him about you…He's not ready for the truth yet . . . He's resting while the others are still out . . . yes . . . thank you, sir."

Wait a second. Was Rafe talking about him? What was the truth he wasn't ready to hear yet? And who exactly was on the other end of that phone call? As much as Omar wanted to answer those questions, he didn't have time to think about it now. He had a stop to make on his way out, and Rafe wouldn't be distracted for much longer.

As quickly as he could, Omar skirted past the open door while Rafe ended the call and clicked off his phone. He ran to a doorway at the end of the hall.

Omar quickly keyed in the code to the door's security lock and snuck inside.

The room he was now in housed much of the state-of-the-art gear the Revolution team used while retrieving Fragments of the 900 board. Anything and everything the team would need was available, from computer tablets to spare board parts. In the center of the room was a platform on which rested a thick glass case. Inside the case, a number of Fragments lay on a black cushion. The artifacts were carefully displayed as a re-construction of the 900 board. Aside from the initial artifacts that the team carried on their person, the case held every part of the mystical board, including the newest acquisition, the truck axle found in Venice. Omar approached the case. He could feel the electromagnetic pull emitting from the Fragments, drawing him closer. A thin tendril of electricity arced from the glowing wheel of his deck to the glass case.

Omar took a deep breath. "It's now or never."

*   *   *

The teenage girl looked over her thick reading glasses at Omar and asked in a slight Columbian accent, "Nervous flyer?"

Omar was 35,000 feet over the Pacific Ocean, sitting in the cramped confines of a 747.

The plane, a connecting redeye flight from Los Angeles to Honolulu, was quite full considering the time of night. Omar had lucked out and found an available seat in coach. He'd used a Revolution company card — given to each of the kids in case of an emergency — to withdraw enough cash to purchase the ticket. Eldrick was already going to be steamed; this act may very well wind up giving the old man a coronary.

"Huh?" Omar looked over at the girl, sitting in a pool of dim light coming from above them.

The teen smiled, closed her book, and indicated Omar's bouncing knee. "You haven't stopped fidgeting since takeoff."

"Oh." Omar put his injured hand on his knee to stop it from moving. "Sorry about that."

"No problem. I'm actually not the best flyer myself. And I can never fall asleep. That's why I always bring my favorite book, as a sercurity blanket." She held up her dog-eared paperback of *The Great Gatsby*. "Distraction is key." She offered her hand. "I'm Lora," she said.

"Omar."

"Well, nice to meet you, Omar."

They shook hands, and Omar blushed. She was about his age, maybe a year older, and attractive.

Her dark, wavy hair was pulled back in a ponytail, and her mocha-colored skin was nearly flawless. Despite the plane cabin's warmth, she wore jeans and a green and black sweater.

"Do you often fly alone?" Lora asked.

"First time," Omar answered. "Do you?"

"Fly alone? Unfortunately, yes. You'd think I'd be okay with it by now, but I still get nervous every time."

The flight attendant breezed past with drinks and snacks. Omar ordered a soda, and quickly downed the beverage. He couldn't risk falling asleep, and needed to stay caffeinated.

"Have you ever been to Hawaii?" Lora asked.

"Yeah. When I was a kid." Under normal circumstances, Omar would cherish the idea of a hot girl chatting him up, but his mind was on other things.

Lora pressed on. "What brings you to the islands?"

"Family emergency," he lied.

"Sorry to hear that. My reason is much more boring. I'm going to see my boyfriend."

"Oh."

Omar leaned back and rested his head against the seat. He imagined what was happening back in Arizona. By now, Eldrick had discovered his absence, and most likely, his GPS watch.

No doubt that despite the time of night, the entire team was awake and trying their hardest to find him. Omar felt a twinge of guilt. He imagined Joey, Amy, and Slider were beyond worried about him. Well, maybe not Slider. They'd probably tried to call him over a hundred times. But he had ditched his phone at the airport so that he couldn't be tracked by the cellular signal. He was on his own.

Just like his vision.

"That's some pretty cool art," Lora whispered. She was pointing at the triangular sketch of the symbol on Omar's wrapped hand.

Omar quickly turned his wrist to hide the image. "Oh, thanks," he said. "It's, uh, it's just a doodle. I was bored."

"I like it," Lora said. "Looks right out of an ancient culture or something."

"Yeah, I guess."

"What does it mean?"

"Heck if I know." *Hopefully by the time I'm done in Hawaii, I'll have some answers, though.*

A soft bing rang throughout the cabin, and the low, soothing voice of the pilot came over the speakers. "Ladies and gentlemen, we are beginning our descent into Honolulu. Flight attendants, prepare for landing."

TRUST SNAKE
BEACH ENERG
COLLECTIVE OMA
EVOLUTION TEA
HAWAII TOMMY T
ENERGY ARTIFAC

8

Man, this place is crawling with tourists.

Omar walked through the terminal at Honolulu International Airport. He skirted visitors in loud floral shirts with enormous cameras hanging around their necks. His backpack was slung over his shoulders, and he carried his skateboard under his arm. Around his neck was a purple lei, a flower necklace given to each passenger on the plane as a customary greeting upon landing. A beautiful, deeply tan woman had placed it around his neck as she pleasantly said, "Aloha."

This wasn't the first time Omar had been to Oahu. He recalled a couple of childhood visits when his family — including Tommy — had come to watch Zeke surf.

The morning sun was just peeking over the horizon, casting an orange dreamsicle glow through the tall windows of the terminal. According to the hand-drawn map in his hands — and his illegible writing — the volcano he was searching for was named Kikaha 'Io. It was located on the state's largest island, Hawaii, which meant Omar was going to have to dig into his cash supply and hop on a puddle-jumper to get there.

Omar was studying his map intently, not looking where he was going, when he collided head-on with someone. His deck clattered to the ground, and the other person's belongings landed at Omar's feet.

"Whoa, I'm sorry," Omar said, cramming the map into his pocket and looking up to see Lora standing there.

"Hey, Omar," she said.

"Lora. I'm so sorry."

"It's okay. I wasn't looking either. I can be such a klutz." She crouched down to gather her things.

"Oh, hey, it was totally my fault. Let me get those for you." Omar crouched beside her, scooping up her tattered paperback and a notebook. As Lora reached over to grab them, the right sleeve of her green sweater slid up to reveal her forearm.

Omar nearly fell backward in shock.

Tattooed on her inner wrist was the image of a black serpent. It slithered in a band around her petite arm. She quickly pulled down her sleeve, trying to cover the tattoo, but it was too late.

"Your ink . . ." Omar trailed off. He was in deeper trouble than he'd thought. He stared into Lora's dark, penetrating eyes. For the first time, he saw the truth in them.

"Well, I guess the cat's out of the bag," Lora said with an impish grin. "A little sooner than I'd hoped."

"Wait a second," Omar said. "You're . . ."

"Yes."

Omar slowly stood. He tried to run, but his feet felt like cement. The Collective had found him. How? He had been careful, had tried so hard to make sure his own team wouldn't be able to track him. But somehow, the Collective was on to him.

Behind Lora, approaching quickly, were three men in sleek black coats and sunglasses. Definitely not tourists, Omar thought. He looked behind him. Four more Collective agents flanked him, teens in black carrying skateboards of their own.

He was surrounded.

The tingle of electricity from his deck, resting on the tile floor beside him, crept up his legs.

He needed to get out of here.

"I know what you're thinking," Lora said. "Please do not make a scene. Just come quietly with us, and you won't get hurt."

Omar's eyes flickered down to the board at his feet.

"You'd be foolish to run, Omar."

"Who said anything about running?" As quick as he could, Omar leaped on his deck, felt the familiar bend of the wood, and pushed off across the tile floor. He left behind twin trails of sapphire electricity in his wake.

Omar darted through the traffic-heavy terminal. He wove around families bouncing with excitement, and newlyweds holding hands. Behind him, Lora shouted, "Don't let him get away!" Omar glanced over his shoulder quickly. The men pursued on foot, and the teens leaped onto their boards and rode after him. They did not care that many of the airport's guests were now aware of the ruckus.

Though he'd barely slept the night before, the intense surge of electricity from the board filled Omar with a renewed sense of power and heightened skills.

Ahead of him, a cluster of travelers waited near a baggage claim carousel. Getting around them was going to be tricky. He'd have to dismount and run past. He'd lose valuable time. Unless . . .

Omar crouched low, wove right, and ollied high into the air. He landed on the metal lip of the carousel, smoothly performing a backside 50-50. Tourists leaped back in alarm. One man, leaning over the carousel to retrieve his luggage from the moving conveyor belt, fell forward onto the track.

"Sorry!" Omar yelled at the man as he zipped past.

Omar reached the end of the carousel, smoothly landing back on the tile, and slid to a stop. He saw the Collective boys through the crowd. They were still on his tail. He whipped around and took off again.

He needed to get out of the building, onto the streets.

One hundred feet ahead of him, Omar saw an airport employee pushing a cart overflowing with luggage toward a set of sliding glass doors. A family of four — the parents wearing ridiculous straw hats, and their children, two girls under ten years of age wearing grass skirts — trailed behind the employee.

Omar was going to have to time his ride perfectly.

Come on, get there, he thought as he crouched low on his board. There was a scuffle behind him, a woman crying out, "How rude!" as the Collective agents elbowed their way through the crowd at the carousel. Omar kept his eyes on the family with the luggage cart.

The airport employee reached the doors, and they slid open just as Omar had hoped. The teen rocketed forward. A surge of blue electricity sparked beneath him. He shot past the family, missing the father, whose straw hat flew off his head as Omar breezed by.

"Wow!" Omar heard one of the little girls cry out. "That boy looks so cool!"

"He should be wearing a helmet," the mother said.

Bigger fish to fry, lady, Omar thought as he carved a hairpin right turn. He was in the airport's loading area. A line of cars were parked along the street and more were crawling past at a low speed. Omar ollied off the curb and streaked across a walkway. He'd officially left the Collective goons in the dust.

Omar skated onto the streets of Honolulu, taking some time to gather his thoughts and let the adrenaline from his confrontation with Lora and the other Collective members drain from him. He was still going to need a flight to the large island if he wanted to track down the Fragment. And he was going to have to do it quickly. His stomach twisted in knots as he thought about the Collective getting their hands on the piece. Sure, his vision had warned him about this, but he had stupidly believed he could change the future.

By mid-morning, Omar had made his way down to the shore. He sat in the shade of a palm tree, near a wooden sign with a tiki god riding a surfboard. The sign read: Tiki Beach. In the water, a number of surfers paddled out into the rolling set of waves. He watched a teen boy riding a small board called a Rocket Fish drop in on a smooth set, expertly performing a series of tight turns before cutting back and gliding toward the shore. Omar used to love the water; he used to hit the beach with Zeke every day. His dad had lovingly called him Shark, a nickname he'd outgrown but still cherished. He could still feel the hot sand between his toes. It made him homesick, made him miss his father even more.

Hot tears began to form in the corners of his eyes. What was he doing? He shouldn't be here, not by himself. He should find a phone, call Eldrick before things got too far out of control.

Omar pushed down the emotions before they overtook him. He carried his board over to a nearby food vendor, a small hut with a thatched roof and a smoking grill. The line was small. As Omar inhaled the intoxicating smell of cooking food, he realized that he hadn't eaten a meal in nearly a whole day. His mouth began to water and his stomach cramped up.

Two teens, a boy with a black fauxhawk and a girl with blonde hair, stood laughing in front of him. As the plump, Samoan man behind the food counter handed off their food, they turned. The boy nearly bumped directly into Omar.

"Whoa!" the boy said. His food wavered in his hands. "Sorry, dude."

"No worries," Omar murmured as the teens walked away.

"That board was pretty sick," Omar heard the girl say. "Either I was seeing things, or it was glowing."

"Glowing? You're so full of it," was her cohort's response.

"What can I get you?" the cook barked across the counter at Omar.

Omar ordered a mahi-mahi burger, paying the man with a few crumpled bills from his Revolution stash. The sloppy, delicious-looking burger was served in mere minutes. Omar snatched up the plastic basket and immediately gouged out a huge bite. It tasted like perfection.

He was walking along a beach promenade, almost done with lunch, when he noticed a black van parked on a nearby street. Its presence immediately put him on edge.

He quickened his pace, looking over his shoulder to see if the van would follow him. Sure enough, it began to roll forward.

"Crap," Omar muttered, dropping the last bit of burger in a trash barrel and breaking out in a run.

A wide set of wooden stairs led up to the street, and a separate sidewalk. Omar took them two at a time. He threw his board in front of him before his feet even reached the cement. He launched himself onto the moving deck, gliding down a hill at a breakneck pace. Ahead, the street ended at a cul-de-sac, but the sidewalk continued into a sprawling beachside park. If he could make it there, where there were no roads, he'd most likely be safe.

A solid thunk came from behind him, as something struck Omar's backpack. He looked back at the van. The side door was open, and a Collective agent leaned out, tranquilizer gun in hand. Omar dug around at his pack and pulled a dart from the canvas.

A three-foot curb leading up to the park loomed in front of him. Omar skated up, snapped the tail of his deck, and leaped up into a backside kickflip. The sapphire-glowing board twirled beneath him as he soared through the air. He landed perfectly, now facing backward and seeing the van.

Pain shot through his right arm. This time, though, it was not from the burn on his hand. It was from the tranq dart sticking out of his bicep.

He felt groggy. The world closed in on him. Swirling black dots swam in the periphery of his vision. The van stuttered to a stop. Three Collective agents rushed out, followed by Lora. Omar fell from his board, almost in slow motion. He landed in the grass, near the base of a towering palm.

He struggled to stay conscious.

It was a battle he quickly lost.

9

He sees them all at once, Fragments in oceans and mountains, in cities and rolling plains of wheat. He wonders why they are where they are. How did they get there? And how can he possibly find them all? The images come at him like pages in a flipbook, overlaying one another until there is nothing but the blinding white. And then he is falling again, off the volcano. He sees the bird high above. He sees the brown and red feather, like the one on Joey's helmet, and he knows it is a Rail. The Rail is not alone. There are others. Two more. A black Crow and the brown plumage of a female Kestrel. His friends. He is not alone; he is part of a family. A new family. He is pulled upward with force, not his body but his essence. He is moving toward Tommy in serpent form.

Then he is Tommy. He is looking down at himself as he plummets. Watches as his arms sprout into wings. As the trio of soaring birds — first the Rail, then the Kestrel and Crow — swoop down to catch him. They will always catch him.

Omar jolted awake, unsure of his whereabouts. It was dark. He let his eyes adjust to the shadows. The blinds in the room had been pulled closed, and the tiniest slivers of daylight bled between their slats. The bed he was sitting on, a thin mattress on a simple metal frame, was the only piece of furniture in the room. The walls were made of bamboo and the high ceiling was thatched. It was a wooden hut.

I have to get out of here. He stood, too quickly, and the dirt floor beneath him felt like the rolling tide of the ocean. He steadied himself, waited until he knew he wouldn't fall on his butt, and ran to the wooden door.

Locked.

He balled his hands into fists, suddenly realizing the wrapping around his right hand was now missing. Using his uninjured hand, he pounded on the door. "Hey!" he shouted. "Let me out of here!" There was no answer. He continued to wail on the door for what felt like an eternity, but no one responded. They either weren't there, or didn't care.

Finally, he gave up. His hand was sore, and he was out of breath from shouting. He slumped onto the bed.

Minutes passed. Then, there was a sound outside, and the door lock was disengaged. It swung open, bringing with it a brilliant blast of daylight. A lone figure stood silhouetted by the glare. Omar squinted, trying to make out who it was.

"We're in the middle of the jungle," came Lora's calm voice. "You can shout all you want, no one will hear you but the birds and the rodents."

"Don't forget the snakes," Omar added through gritted teeth.

Lora entered the room, flanked by two mean-looking Collective goons carrying taser batons.

Lora laughed. "Nice. You're funny, just like your brother."

"My . . .?" Omar couldn't finish the question.

Instead, someone finished it for him.

"Bro!" A smiling Tommy stood in the doorframe. "How's it hangin'?!"

Omar's stomach sank like a dead weight. He was here. Alive and in the flesh. Seeing Tommy in his vision was one thing. But coming face to face with the best friend he'd thought was dead? He couldn't find a way to wrap his brain around it.

"You look great, by the way," Tommy said, playfully clapping Omar on the shoulder. "Like a real man now, and not that wimpy kid back in SoCal who couldn't land an Imperial 5-0 to save his life."

"How are you here?" Omar asked. "I saw you . . ."

"Float to the bottom of the ocean after you introduced your foot to my scuba mask?"

"Um, yeah."

"What can I say?" Tommy smiled. "I'm a survivor. That really stung, though." He massaged his chin for emphasis. "But you know what?"

"What?"

"I forgive you." Tommy's words sounded completely sincere. "Because that's what family does. They forgive one another."

He sat beside Omar on the bed, and motioned to one of the Collective agents, who handed him a silver canteen. Tommy held it out to Omar. "Drink?"

Omar's mouth felt like a desert, and his tongue like a scrap of sandpaper. He snatched the canteen from Tommy, and guzzled the fresh, cool water. It trickled down his chin and soaked into his T-shirt.

"Why?" Omar wiped his mouth with a dirty forearm.

"Excuse me?"

"My family — Zeke — loved you. Why would you betray us? How could you kill him?!"

"Oh. That." Tommy sighed, biting his lower lip and thinking about it. "Omar, I loved your old man like he was my own father. I would have done anything for him."

"Yeah, right."

"No, it's true. I lived my whole life with this gnawing, scratching feeling inside. Like no matter what I ever did, I'd always be evil. But Zeke, man, he didn't look at me like that. He saw me as . . . as a kid."

Tommy stood. He paced the floor as he continued speaking. "At least, that's what I thought. Dude, I can't even tell you how badly I wanted to be you. You were happy. You were loved. I lay awake at night, envious of you and your family, hoping that Zeke felt the same way about me as he did about you. Because I needed a dad, I needed to be somebody's son. But then . . ." His eyes grew sad, but Omar sensed a deep anger behind the hurt. ". . . I found out he knew."

"Knew what?" Omar quietly asked.

"Zeke knew about what I could become. And do you know what he did about it?"

Omar shook his head.

"Nothing," Tommy spat.

"He didn't keep me close because he loved me," said Tommy. "He kept me close because he feared me. His whole Revolution was afraid of me."

"That's bull! Dad loved you, and you know it."

"Stop!" Tommy jabbed a finger so close to Omar's face, it nearly touched his nose. "Don't say that. Don't lie to your best friend."

Behind Tommy, a Collective agent entered the hut and whispered in Lora's ear.

"I was so angry," Tommy continued. "I decided to stop fighting. To search out the Collective and face my destiny head-on. They told me where Zeke was surfing, and I paddled out after him. I only meant to scare him, but . . . well, I guess I got lucky, huh?"

A wave of anger passed through Omar. He leaped to his feet, ready to fight Tommy here and now for what he'd done to Zeke. The two Collective goons moved quickly, though. Before Omar had taken a step, they blocked his path to Tommy. One of them, the man Omar recognized as the shooter back in the van, jammed his baton into Omar's side. A small current of electricity coursed through him. His muscles cramped as he fell back onto the bed.

"Tommy?" Lora's soft voice asked.

Tommy took a deep breath. "Yes?"

"It's getting late. We really need to be going if we want to reach the site before sundown."

"Okay." Tommy walked over to the bed. "Come on." He grabbed Omar by the arm and yanked him to his feet.

"Where are we going?" Omar asked. He was still recovering from the taser blast.

"Where do you think?" Tommy dug into his back jeans pocket and removed the uncoiled wrapping from Omar's hand. Tommy displayed the ancient symbol scribbled on the bandage. "We're going to find this."

10

The blazing sun beat down from a cloudless sky and burned the back of Omar's neck. He was drenched in sweat, his soaked T-shirt clinging to his chest. They had been hiking for over an hour, first through the jungle and then across the jagged base of Kikiha 'lo. They walked in a straight line — Tommy, Lora, two Collective goons, and then Omar. Behind him were two more agents, including his taser-happy friend. Slung over the massive man's shoulder was Omar's backpack, and in his hand was a heavy-duty nylon bag containing Omar's skateboard. Tommy had instructed the agent to keep the board away from Omar at all costs.

The winding path crept upward. In front of them was the volcano from Omar's vision.

Omar couldn't believe he was here, that he would soon be climbing — then falling — from the towering mountainside before him.

The caravan reached a small plateau overlooking the ocean, and Tommy instructed them to stop. "Ten minutes. Rest and drink. We're almost there."

A pocked-face agent led Omar to a nearby boulder, where the teen willingly sat. His legs were like Jell-O. He was so used to the restorative energy supplied by the Fragment in his board. Without it, he was just a normal teen.

Tommy walked over, looking past Omar at the crashing waves. "Looks like killer surf weather today," he said.

Omar couldn't take Tommy's smug, easy-going attitude. He stood up and began to walk away.

"You haven't asked me how I knew you'd be here yet," Tommy called after him.

Omar stopped and turned. "It doesn't really matter," he said. "Let's just get this over with."

Tommy ignored Omar, instead holding out his clenched right fist. Suddenly, a burst of red electricity sparked and engulfed his hand. He opened his fist, palm up. Resting amidst the crimson glow was a truck axle. Just like the one Omar had found in Venice.

"That's . . ." Omar's voice trailed off.

"A Fragment. Yes."

Omar felt the power drawing him closer. He moved toward it, reached out his hand. The axle flickered blue, then burned red as Tommy closed his fist again.

"We found it in Beijing," he said. "Beneath a fourteenth century temple, built during the Ming Dynasty."

Omar's eyes darted over to the hulking Collective agent, and the backpack still hanging off his shoulder.

"Since it's been in my possession, the Fragment has gifted me with visions. It showed me this place, and it showed me a symbol. The very same one you drew, Omar." Tommy looked Omar in the eye. "It told me you would be here. It told me that I would kill you."

The two teens stood facing one another, neither of them blinking, neither of them retreating.

Finally, Tommy smiled. "Let's go face our destiny, bro," he said, then turned and began to climb the volcano once more.

*   *   *

"This is it."

They stood in the shade of an outcropping of rocks. A dark tunnel led into the volcano, nearly hidden by overhanging brush and vines.

A black snake slithered out of the cave and, fittingly, over Tommy's hiking boot. Its presence didn't faze the teen at all.

Instead, Tommy ducked his head inside the cave entrance, opening his hand and using the Fragment's red glow like a flashlight. "Omar," he called out, his voice echoing. "You first, bud. Come on."

Omar climbed into the tunnel. He felt the temperature immediately drop. The rock walls were cool to the touch.

Using the red electric glow at his back as a guide, Omar began to maneuver through the tunnel. Tommy was right behind him, with Lora and the rest of the Collective members trailing them.

Climbing was difficult in skate shoes. More than once, Omar slipped on loose rocks and nearly fell. Every so often, the tunnel would end in a pile of fallen, broken boulders, and the group would need to scale them to continue upward. Omar's injury to his right hand made this difficult, but he pressed on.

When they reached a split in the tunnel, Omar was unsure which direction to take. He noticed Tommy examining the smooth surface of the rock wall to his left, running his hand over something etched in the stone. Omar backtracked and looked over his shoulder.

"Amazing," Tommy said under his breath.

The glyphs on the wall were ancient, nearly hidden by moss and cobwebs. Omar recognized some of them from the inscription beneath the symbol in his vision. It was a signpost marking the passage and directing them to the left tunnel in the fork.

"This way, I guess," Omar said, taking the cave to his left and proceeding into the dark.

The glyphs appeared at several times during their ascent, like breadcrumbs left to guide them. After much climbing — and after getting hit in the face with a couple of thick, moldy cobwebs, Omar saw light in the distance. With renewed energy, he climbed toward it.

Omar squinted as he exited the cracked cave and back out into the late afternoon sunshine. He stumbled forward, twisting his ankle on a piece of black and broken lava rock. The sight of the rock reminded Omar that, despite the fact that the volcano was dormant, molten-hot liquid was churning deep below their feet.

Tommy and the Collective members staggered out into the daylight. Lora offered Tommy a canteen, which he, in turn, produced for Omar. "How are you holding up?" Tommy asked.

Omar took a drink, then thrust the canteen back into Tommy's chest. "Stop acting like you care," he said.

They may have been back out in the sun, but they were still surrounded on all sides by rock. A small path fifty yards ahead led up the jagged rock face and to a massive plateau.

The red glow emanating from Tommy's Fragment reached out toward the path, tendrils of electricity urging to break free.

"This way," Tommy said, taking over the lead.

Up, up, up they climbed. The sloped rock wall was difficult, but finally they reached the top.

The view was awe-inspiring. Before them was the entire island of Hawaii. The coastline cut a ragged course along the horizon. Lush, rolling green foliage blanketed the earth. In the distance, hazy as a mirage, were the towering buildings of what must be the city of Hilo. Despite the circumstances, Omar was amazed by the sight.

At the edge of the plateau was a steep cliff. Before it was an unusual outcropping of rocks, a manmade, circular structure of stone. In its center, a rectangular boulder jutted into the sky.

Tommy and Omar walked together toward the site.

Omar saw it first. Etched at the base of the towering stone was the symbol from his vision.

They had found the Fragment.

"Quickly! Come on!" Tommy beckoned to the Collective agents trailing them. The quartet of baddies rushed to his side. "I can feel it. It must be under the rock."

The agent carrying Omar's backpack and board shrugged them off. They landed in the dirt, a plume of dust rising off them. He abandoned them to assist the others as they began to push the towering stone.

At first, it would not budge. They pressed their shoulders against the rock, grunting with exertion.

Omar watched them as he slowly inched toward his backpack, and the surprise contained within it. He was just about there when Lora's voice piped up behind him.

"What do you think you're doing?" she asked.

Omar was hit in the back with a blast from her taser. The current made the hair on his neck and arms rise. He dropped to his knees.

He had one chance. He was going to have to use all his strength, but if he wanted to get out of here alive, he needed to try. As fast as his tired, cramping legs could move, Omar scrambled forward on his hands and knees. He reached his backpack, snatched it up, and jumped to his feet before Lora could react and taze him again.

"Tommy!" Lora yelled.

11

Omar stumbled, stood, unzipped his pack and rooted around inside it. *Where are you?* he thought as his hand dug deeper. He was suddenly hit with a sense of panic and dread. It was gone. They had taken it.

And then his fingers found it, the lead-lined box at the very bottom of the pack.

"Stop!" Tommy cried. A blast of energy rocketed toward Omar, hitting him full-on in the chest. He fell backward, landing on his butt. Tommy was running toward him, the Fragment heightening his speed.

Omar pulled the box from his backpack. He unlatched it, opened it . . . and was hit with a blinding blast of blue light.

The truck axle he'd recovered in Italy shot out of the box and into Omar's hand. It washed away his fatigue and cleared his mind.

"Two can play that game," Omar said. From a sitting position, he thrust the Fragment out in front of him, sending a brilliant trail of blue energy at Tommy. Tommy was caught off-guard. The blast hit him in the shoulder, spinning him around.

Omar needed to escape, before his vision came true and he fell to his death. He spied the duffel bag containing his board. If he could reach it, and make a mad dash for the tunnel, he could survive. Live to fight another day.

He ran to the duffel bag. Behind him, Tommy staggered to his feet. He aimed a second energy blast at Omar. It sizzled over the teen's head, hitting the stone tower instead. The Collective agents gathered around the stone were tossed like ragdolls from the rock. The stone cracked down the center and, to Omar's surprise, it split in two and fell to the ground.

"I see it!" Lora cried out, rushing to the site. The rocks around her were still enveloped with red electricity. She slid to her knees and began digging the soft earth beneath the stone.

Omar stopped dead in his tracks.

He wanted to flee, but the Fragment would not let him. It coursed through him, kept him rooted in place. He watched as Lora removed a metal box from the ground. It was battered, rusted, and caked with clumps of earth.

"I have it, Tommy!" she yelled, turning and waving the box in the air. "I have the artifact!"

The box suddenly shook in her hand. It lifted out of her grip and into the air, where it hovered high above them. Omar suddenly could not control his Fragment as it slipped from his fingers and was drawn into the sky, too. He looked to Tommy. The red-glowing truck axle was doing the same. Tommy was struggling to hold onto it, his toes scraping the ground as he lifted into the air with the piece.

The lid of the box flew open, and two glowing items escaped. They remained in the air as the box clattered to the rocky ground. Omar couldn't quite make out what the Fragments were yet.

The blue axle truck buzzed like a magnet toward the items. Finally relinquishing his hold, Tommy dropped to the ground as his Fragment did the same. The two boys watched as the truck axles collided in a burst of energy. The truck halves fused together as the other two items locked into place around them.

Omar could see them now. He knew what they were: the truck's baseplate and kingpin.

Finally whole, the skateboard truck erupted in white light. Then, it plummeted to the ground, sizzling and blackening the earth around it.

Omar looked at Tommy. Tommy stared back. It was like a Western showdown. They both knew exactly what the other was thinking.

OMAR
❧ VERSUS ❧
TOMMY

12

It's happening. My vision is coming true.

As he began to fall, Omar's fingers searched out and found a crack in the sheer face of the cliff. He dug them into the rock with all his might, jolting to a stop. Pain coursed through his arm as it supported his entire weight. His legs kicked around for a toehold, finding a lip in the rock face and easing the burden on his arm.

It was eerily silent hanging in the air. A strong wind whipped at him, trying to pry him from his perilous grasp. Omar fought the urge to look down.

He lost. The cliff dropped about a hundred feet before turning into a steep hillside speckled with trees and shrubs.

Even if he survived the initial fall, Omar was certain he would tumble all the way down to the base of the volcano.

A bird's screech cut through the quiet. Omar looked up to see his namesake and protector, a grebe, circling high above. *How long has the bird been there?* he wondered. The grebe was not alone. A second bird, small as a pinprick against the blue sky, flew behind it. As it grew larger and closer, Omar began to hear the distant, steady thrum of helicopter rotors, and the truth hit him: the grebe's companion was a bird of a different sort; it was not an animal, but a sleek Black Hawk helicopter. A very familiar one.

Omar threw his head back and released a loud, throaty exclamation of relief. His friends were coming to rescue him.

Moments later, the Black Hawk roared over the top of the volcano, circling back around and hovering where Omar could see it. Three black coils of rope dropped from the bird and landed on the plateau. Omar saw the blurred image of Joey, Slider, and Amy glide from the helicopter to the cliff.

As the trio landed safely, a blast of red light erupted into the sky, heading directly for the helicopter and forcing the Black Hawk to bank right.

The crimson shot narrowly missed hitting the bird as it disappeared around the cone of the volcano.

Omar's fingers ached and cramped; he could not hold on much longer. Above him, Omar could hear voices calling out to one another, the crack of rocks splitting. He desperately wanted to be up there, to help his friends. Tommy was too powerful for them; Omar needed to reason with him, to try to speak to whatever part of his friend remained inside Tommy's cold heart.

But he couldn't. Every last bit of Omar's strength had washed out of him. This was it. He had made it this far, but his vision was going to come true. He closed his eyes, willing himself to hold on. His fingers quivered. They slid closer to the edge of the crevasse, until just his fingertips clutched the rock.

And then he fell.

A strong hand grasped his wrist, and Omar jerked to a stop.

He peeled his eyes open to find Amy holding onto him. She was rappelling down the side of the cliff. A harness was strapped around her waist, and she clenched her jaw. The blue electric glow of her Fragment coursed down her arm and into Omar.

"You didn't think we'd let you fall, did you?" she asked through gritted teeth. A smile played on her lips.

Omar found a jutting rock for a toehold as Amy locked a carabiner and a second length of rope on his belt for safety. With Amy's assistance, the two teens scaled back up the sheer face of the cliff.

When they reached the top, Joey — who had been belaying for Amy like he had back at the facility — ran over and pulled Omar back onto solid ground.

"What are you just hanging around for, O?" Joey asked with a grin.

"Haha," Omar said, doubling over. He was weak. He needed to get his board back and find his Fragment.

"Good to see you in one piece, man," Joey said, lightly punching Omar on the shoulder.

Omar scanned the plateau. Tommy was the only Collective member left; the others, including Lora, must have abandoned him and retreated down the tunnel. Tommy stood in the middle of the clearing, the scarlet energy still strongly emanating from the full 900 truck in his grip. Slider was weaving across the rocky surface on his skateboard. The glowing blue of his Fragment tail kept his ride smooth on the unsteady terrain. Tommy directed a blast at the boarder, but Slider kicked into a fluid, but difficult hardflip, and the crimson shot obliterated the stone ground beneath his airborne feet and board, leaving a crater in its wake.

Omar saw the nylon bag with his board inside. It
was twenty feet away. He stepped toward it, but his
weak legs buckled under him and he fell to his knees.
Whatever lingering bit of strength he had was zapped.
He needed . . .

"My board . . ." he said, pointing to the black duffel
bag. Joey understood at once, rushing over and plucking
the black bag off the ground. A red current breezed
over his head as he ran back to Omar and Amy. Joey
unzipped the duffel, presenting the skateboard and its
crackling glow to Omar.

"Stay radical," Omar whispered as the cobalt
electricity coursed from the board into his hands. The
surge of energy was just what he needed; he hopped to
his feet, his deck still in his hands.

A thin streak of sapphire danced across the dry
air, zig-zagging to the necklace — and the Fragment
— laced around Joey's neck. Omar had never seen the
surprising sight, but it gave him an idea.

"Dylan!" Amy screamed. Omar whipped his head up.
Slider had been struck by one of Tommy's blasts, and
had bailed off his board. He crawled on his hands and
knees toward his deck as Tommy, his back to Omar and
his friends, stepped toward him.

"Yo, Tommy!" Omar called out.

Tommy stopped dead in his tracks.

He slowly turned to face Omar. An evil smile lit up his face. "Well, well, well," he said. "And here I thought you'd be somersaulting down the volcano right about now."

"Spread out on either side of me, and dig out your Fragments," Omar told Joey and Amy in a low voice. The two teens did as he directed, side-stepping quickly and beginning to flank Tommy.

Tommy lifted his hand. The truck burned in his palm like an ember from a dying campfire.

"Having second thoughts?" Tommy asked. "You've seen what it can do, what power we can wield. Come on, Omar. You can't tell me you aren't enticed by this."

And he was. Despite everything he'd been through, everything he'd seen, the thought of harnessing a power as ultimate as the one emitted by the 900 board was very enticing. But that wasn't the Revolution. They were a team. They worked together.

On Omar's left, Joey was removing his Fragment necklace from around his neck. Amy, on Omar's right, held her shard of the 900 board tightly in her fist. Omar held his deck in front of him. The power radiating from it was stronger in the crimson truck's presence than it ever had been before.

It took nearly all his strength to contain it. A quick look at his friends confirmed that they, too, were experiencing the same feeling.

A crackling burst of energy erupted from Omar's wheel Fragment, blasting its way toward Joey. Another shot out toward Amy. Each blue bolt connected with its target, the other Fragments, creating a deep blue semicircle around Tommy.

"Dylan, come on!" Amy shouted into the hum of electricity. Slider, still reeling from the attack by Tommy, scooped up his board. Its tail was already glowing blue; as he held it aloft, its shade deepened.

"What are you doing?!" Tommy yelled. For the first time, Omar saw fear in his former friend's eyes.

The current, begun by Omar's board, extended through Joey and Amy's Fragments and connected with Slider's, enclosing Tommy in an azure circle. The thrum emitted by the electric field was nearly deafening.

For a moment, nothing happened. To Tommy's surprise, the truck began to crackle in his hand. It rose into the air. Once more, he tried to cling to it, to hold onto its power. Its crimson color washed away.

"No!" Tommy yelled as beams of electricity sparked from the Revolution members' artifacts and arced toward the pale red truck.

The metal truck flashed a brief, brilliant white against the sky. A thunderous clap of sound rippled from the Fragment, knocking the four Revolution members to the ground.

And then it was silent.

The blue energy field was gone.

The crimson truck was once more a piece of scratched metal. It lay near the outstretched, open hand of an unconscious Tommy.

Omar coughed. He sat up, unsure that his legs could support him. He saw each of his friends rising to their feet, brushing the dirt and dust off their clothes. They were all right.

He lay his head back down on the ground, staring up into the cloudless sky.

"You okay, Omar!?" he heard Joey yell.

He offered a thumbs-up in response.

A shadow passed across the sun. Omar squinted as the Black Hawk helicopter flew overhead, then back to pick them up.

13

"How did you know?!"

Omar didn't hear Amy's question. He was staring from his seat to the cargo hold area in the rear of the Black Hawk, where Tommy's unconscious body lay on a blanket. His wrists and ankles were tied with zip line.

"Omar!?" Amy shouted over the sound of the engine.

He looked up at her.

"How did you know that would happen? With the Fragments?" she asked again.

He shrugged. "I didn't. But I remembered something Tommy told me: Alone, the Fragments are powerful. Together, they're unstoppable."

His gaze flickered over to the cockpit, and the co-pilot seat occupied by a very angry Eldrick. The leader of the Revolution had not said a word to Omar since they'd boarded; it was going to be a long ride home.

"How did you guys find me?" Omar asked.

Joey smiled. "Your art project," he answered. "I remembered seeing the drawings of Hawaii, but they weren't there when we did a search. Just a couple of pin holes in the wall."

"Well . . . thanks," Omar said. "You really risked your lives for me."

Slider shrugged. "Ain't that what family's for?"

The helicopter banked left, and Omar took a moment to look out the window. Far below them, the waves of the Pacific Ocean crashed along the Hawaiian shore. A number of surfers paddled out, ready to drop in on a beautiful set before the sun went down. Omar thought about his family. His father dead. His mother alone and uncertain of her son's whereabouts.

His best friend — his brother — lost to him. And while his heart hurt when thinking of them, Omar knew he was going to be all right. He had the Revolution. He had friends, mentors. A different family.

And they would never let him fall.

Tommy Goff_
CODE NAME: TOMMY

AGE: 16

HOMETOWN: San Diego, CA

SPORT: Skateboarding

INTERESTS: Singing, Rock Music

BIO: There was a time when all Tommy Goff wanted to do was rip up the half-pipe at Billy's Board Shop or carve along Seacoast Drive with his best 'brah' Omar Grebes. The boys were inseparable, like two sides of the same coin. That was before Tommy's dad bailed on their family. Before he was tossed in juvie for shoplifting and graffiti tagging. Before he was betrayed by Omar's father Zeke, and told his destiny by the shadowy Collective. Now, the lanky, muscular Tommy is a powerful agent for the evil organization. He's reckless and defiant, a wild card with one motive: fulfilling his destiny and stopping the Revolution for good.

STORY SETTING: Hawaii

LOCATING...

ABOUT TONY HAWK

TONY HAWK is the most famous and influential skateboarder of all time. In the 1980s and 1990s, he was instrumental in skateboarding's transformation from fringe pursuit to respected sport. After retiring from competitions in 2000, Tony continues to skate demos and tour all over the world.

He is the founder, President, and CEO of Tony Hawk Inc., which he continues to develop and grow. He is also the founder of the Tony Hawk Foundation, which works to create skateparks and empower youth in low income communities.

TONY HAWK WAS THE FIRST SKATEBOARDER TO LAND THE 900 TRICK, A 2.5 REVOLUTION (900 DEGREES) AERIAL SPIN, PERFORMED ON A SKATEBOARD RAMP.

ABOUT THE AUTHOR_

BRANDON TERRELL is a Saint Paul-based writer and filmmaker. He has worked on television commercials and independent feature films for almost a decade. He has also written dozens of comic books and children's books. When not writing, Brandon enjoys watching movies, reading, baseball, and spending time with his wife Jen and their son Alex.

AUTHOR Q & A_

Q: WHEN DID YOU DECIDE TO BECOME A WRITER?

A: I've been writing and telling stories all of my life. I still have notebooks filled with childhood mysteries I wrote that were inspired by *The Hardy Boys* and *Encyclopedia Brown*. I love the idea of engaging a reader by finding an unexpected way to tell a story. It's been a lifelong passion of mine.

Q: DESCRIBE YOUR APPROACH TO THE TONY HAWK'S 900 REVOLUTION SERIES.

A: My approach always starts with the characters, and trying to find new and exciting ways for them to showcase their extreme talents, while still telling a story that packs an emotional punch. Then I try to imagine locations that are visually interesting as well, places where the Revolution team will be out of their element. While I'm not a globe-trotting traveler myself, some of the locations I've written about are places where I've visited at one time or another. What's fascinating about the series is that it blends multiple genres (mystery, action, science fiction, romance, etc.) all in one book, so the story possibilities are endless!

TONY HAWK'S

900 revolution

TONY HAWK'S 900 REVOLUTION, VOL. 5: AMPLIFIED

As a new chapter begins, the first four members of the Revolution team — Omar, Dylan, Amy, and Joey — search for next piece of Tony Hawk's powerful 900 skateboard. Their journey takes them to the American Midwest, where a rock-n-roll teen named Wren tunes in to the mysterious Fragment's location. Unfortunately, when another gang of teens, known as the Collective, follows them on their quest, the dangers are suddenly amplified.

TONY HAWK'S 900 REVOLUTION VOL. 6: TUNNEL VISION

As the team finds more pieces of t 900 skateboard, the skills of ea member are suddenly magnifi For Omar Grebes, this surge power creates a flood of psyc visions about the locations the Fragments and the ori of their mysterious powers. H determined to find the rest of t missing pieces as fast as possib Unfortunately, Omar's tun vision quickly leads to whirlwind of trouble for the tea

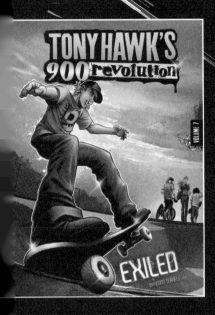

TONY HAWK'S 900 REVOLUTION, VOL. 7: EXILED

Every time the Revolution team finds another piece of the mysterious 900 skateboard, a gang of troublesome teens, known as the Collective, is close behind — and another encounter could be deadly! Omar, Dylan, Amy, and Joey suspect that one of them must be a double-crossing snitch. Soon, these suspicions begin to splinter the Revolution. Only one solution can save the team and their vital quest — send the main suspect into exile!

TONY HAWK'S 900 REVOLUTION, VOL. 8: LOCKDOWN

With Dylan Crow in exile and others on lockdown, the Revolu team is falling apart fast — and t enemies are picking up the pie With each new Fragment, the g of troublesome teens, known as Collective, grows more powe And, when Elliot Addison, a member of the Collective, steals Revolution's cache of Fragments hope seems lost. If the team can't themselves together, the Revolu might be overthrown by

Amy jumped at the sound of Rafe's voice. She turned to see the Revolution mentor standing alongside Omar and Joey. In one hand, Rafe held Dylan's backpack. In his other hand was a device, about the size of a smartphone.

"Care to explain?" Rafe asked, waving the device.

"What is it?" Amy asked.

"We don't know," Omar said. "It looks like a tracking signal."

"But we know where it came from," Joey added.

Rafe turned the device in his hand. Etched into the metallic side was an insignia, the image of a black and gold hawk clutching a lightning bolt in one talon and a sword in the other. Behind the bird was a globe, with latitude and longitude lines etched in red.

Amy had seen the insignia before, as a patch worn by a group of Collective agents she'd encountered back in Colorado.

"Omar found this in your bag, Slider," Rafe said. "I'm going to ask you one more time, son, where did this device come from?"

Dylan said nothing. He clenched his fists, standing alone against the rest of the Revolution team.

"Silence will only incriminate you further," Rafe continued.

"Nothing I can say will make you change your minds," Dylan's defeated voice finally answered. "And I'm not your son."

"Dylan, stop being so stubborn and tell them it's not true," Amy pleaded. "Tell them what you told me."

Dylan shook his head. "They don't care."

Rafe passed the device and pack to Joey, then dug his phone out of his pocket. He made a quick call, speaking in Spanish. A moment later, Felipe pulled his van out of the parking lot and onto the street, near the group.

Rafe walked over to Dylan. "Let's make this easy, Slider," he said, holding out his hands. Dylan kicked the tail of his board, sending it flying up into the air where he could snatch it up. Tendrils of blue electricity coursed from the board. They sparked and died as Dylan passed the deck over to Rafe.

"I'm sorry it has to be like this," Rafe said. "You were an important member of the Revolution, Slider."

"Bite me," was Dylan's crass response.

Read more in the next adventure of . . .

Tony Hawk's 900 Revolution

TONY HAWK'S
900 revolution

www.TonyHawkReadingRevolution.com